BOIL LINE

orca sports

BOIL LINE

M.J. McISAAC

ORCA BOOK PUBLISHERS

Library and Archives Canada Cataloguing in Publication

Title: Boil line / M.J. McIsaac.
Names: McIsaac, M.J., 1986– author.
Series: Orca sports.

Description: Series statement: Orca sports

Identifiers: Canadiana (print) 20190065702 | Canadiana (ebook) 20190065710 | ISBN 9781459818439 (softcover) | ISBN 9781459818446 (PDF) | ISBN 9781459818453 (EPUB)

Classification: LCC PS8625.I837 B65 2019 | DDC jC813/.6—dc23

Library of Congress Control Number: 2019934027
Simultaneously published in Canada and the United States in 2019

Summary: In this high-interest novel for young readers, Nate investigates the disappearance of a river-kayaking guide.

Orca Book Publishers is committed to reducing the consumption of nonrenewable resources in the making of our books. We make every effort to use materials that support a sustainable future.

Orca Book Publishers gratefully acknowledges the support for its publishing programs provided by the following agencies: the Government of Canada, the Canada Council for the Arts and the Province of British Columbia through the BC Arts Council and the Book Publishing Tax Credit.

Edited by Tanya Trafford
Cover photograph by istock.com/EXTREME-PHOTOGRAPHER
Author photo by Crystal Jones

ORCA BOOK PUBLISHERS
orcabook.com

Printed and bound in Canada.

22 21 20 19 • 4 3 2 1

Chapter One

When the river churns to boiling, it becomes something else–something alive, something solid and angry. Like a thousand giant, heavy fists pounding your body. It fights you. Fights to squash you down. To bury you in the frothing white. Pushing and pulling until you think it's going to rip you apart. Until you think it's going to swallow you up. But you can't let it. You have to fight back. You have to show the river your worth.

If you're lucky, it might just decide to spit you back out.

Like it did me.

Mike stood beside me, his hand on my shoulder as we looked out over the canyon. The rapids thundered below us. I was twelve and had just started my first year at Camp Clearwater.

"Nate, do you want to head back?" he asked.

Mike knew about me. Mr. Evans, the camp director, had told him what had happened to me. Mom and Mr. Evans thought it was important that my "designated camp buddy" be aware, in case I freaked out.

Last summer the Starling River tried to drown me.

"I'm okay," I replied. My voice was practically a whisper. Because I was *not* okay. As I looked down at the white water, my knees felt ready to buckle.

Mike squeezed my shoulder gently. Then he leaned over the edge for a better look. "I just want to say, Nate, I think it's pretty brave of you to be here."

"You do?"

He nodded. “A lot of people wouldn’t want to get near the river again after going through what you went through. I bet I wouldn’t have the guts.”

I bet he would. Mike is one of the best paddlers at Camp Clearwater. Then again, what happened to me on the river would never happen to someone like Mike. The river loves him.

“Hey!” a voice barked behind us.

Mike and I turned around to see the other campers dropping their backpacks and collapsing onto tree trunks and rocks. The younger ones wore green shirts, like me. First year. The older kids, like Mike, wore blue shirts. Fourth year.

One of the girls folded her arms across her chest. “We’ve been walking for hours. What is this, a hiking camp?”

“This, Mercy Chapman,” said Mr. Evans, standing at the edge of the canyon, “is how we get to know the river.” He had been leading us on a hike along the edge of the Starling for what felt like hours. Said it was tradition. That every Camp Clearwater camper went through it their first year.

The girl, Mercy, rolled her eyes. "It's water. I think we get it."

"You do, huh?" Mr. Evans shrugged and pointed down to the water. "Then I suppose you know what that is down there?"

"Rapids," said Mercy.

"Not just any rapids," Mike said. "That's the Nebula."

"Correct, Mike!" said Mr. Evans. "They're the toughest rapids Camp Clearwater rides. If you green shirts make it through all your levels, then in four years you'll all be blue shirts. As fifth-years, as red shirts, you get to take on your final challenge, the Nebula."

Mercy's eyebrows went up. The other kids began to murmur to each other, clearly excited by the idea.

Not me. Taking a raft down any rapids, let alone the Nebula, instantly made my armpits damp with sweat. And that's why my mom had sent me to Camp Clearwater. She said that if I could learn how to navigate the Starling, then I would no longer be afraid of it. And I was tired of being afraid.

"Since you think you know the river so well, Mercy Chapman," said Mr. Evans, "then why don't you tell us what class the Nebula is."

Mercy looked at her feet.

One of the green-shirt boys, with curly dark hair and wearing socks that didn't match, raised his hand. "Class Four."

Mr. Evans pointed a finger at him. "Right you are, Owen Barry. Class Four. Down there you'll face powerful waters, narrow passes, jutting rocks. Only our best paddlers can handle a Class Four. And they all started learning the river the same way you are learning it today. On this hike. Pay attention, and someday you'll earn your blue shirt."

"And then do we get one of those too?" Mercy pointed at Mike's ankle, at the black handle jutting out of his left sock. Mike grabbed the handle and pulled out a black knife, the blade sheathed in a plastic cover.

My mouth gaped open. I didn't think my mom knew about the knife part of all this. I was pretty sure she wouldn't like it.

Mike caught me staring and, with a grin, handed the knife to me. It was small and light, but the blade looked very sharp.

"You do," said Mr. Evans. "A river knife like that is essential gear for a kayaker. If your boat flips and some part of you gets caught in a rope, you need to be able to cut yourself free."

If your boat flips. I handed it back.

"You like it?" Mike asked.

I shrugged.

He tucked the knife back into his sock. "Brings me luck, this knife," he said. "It's going to get me through the Nebula this year."

I glanced back down at the raging current and swallowed, glad I didn't have to take on the Nebula yet.

"Is there a Class Five?" Mercy asked.

Mr. Evans rubbed his neck, his lips pressed tightly together. "There is. A Class Five is an extremely violent ride. Obstructions, steep chutes, big holes. We do have some right here on the Starling." He pointed past where the Nebula ended to the calmer waters we could see downstream. "A couple miles down that way is what we call the Black Hole. Class Five. Not even our most experienced rafters would want to tackle the Black Hole. Which is why you need to know the river. So you can avoid dangerous situations."

"Do you know anyone who's been through it?" Mercy asked. "The Black Hole?"

Mike's hand fell on my shoulder again as Mr. Evans glanced in my direction. "One person."

Chapter Two

Four years later...

The night is black. Even out here, so far from the city, the stars refuse to shine. As it should be, I guess. On a night like this.

From the car, I can see the flicker of candle flame by the water's edge. The orange and yellow lights do nothing to light up the darkness of the Starling. Even the river is somber tonight. I step out of the car, my feet crunching on the gravel. I stretch my legs, stiff from the three-hour drive, and take a deep breath in. The air smells like juniper and cedar and the clean, fishy musk of the river. The smells of Camp Clearwater.

"I just hope Mr. Evans doesn't close the camp," Mercy says, climbing out of the driver's side. It's still hard to believe Mercy has her driver's license already. I haven't even tried to get my learner's.

Owen climbs out behind me, slamming the door. "Seriously, Mercy. Is that all you can think about? Tonight?"

"What? I'm just saying, this is supposed to be the year we take on the Nebula. I don't want to have to miss it."

"Keep it down," Owen hisses, flapping his arms. "Someone might hear you."

"I'm just saying..." Mercy grumbles.

"Well, don't," snaps Owen. "Tonight's not about you or the Nebula. Tonight's about Mike. Right, Nate?"

I nod and turn away from them, heading toward the group gathered by the water's edge, toward the glow of candles. Tonight is about Mike.

"I know what tonight's about," I hear Mercy mutter behind me. "I drove us out here, didn't I? You're welcome, by the way."

Walking up to the crowd that has gathered, I recognize a lot of faces–faces I've come to know well after four years. Faces I'm used to seeing lit up with smiles. There are no smiles tonight.

Sharlene Clarins, one of the park rangers, reaches into the shoebox she's carrying and hands me an unlit white candle. She hands one to Owen and Mercy too and then moves on as we make our way deeper into the crowd.

There are a lot of people here. The entire population of Guilford Falls, Mike's and Camp Clearwater's hometown, has come out. Alana, one of the counselors who's been here since I was a green shirt, folds up her empty shoebox–she's out of candles. She hands tissue to Molly, the lifeguard, as Chef Jake rubs her arm. Bella, Lucy and Declan G–third-years–stand huddled together over their little flames, crying quietly.

Raina Madero, the camp's assistant director, stands over by the water's edge, her clipboard clutched to her chest like always. She's in director mode, running through whatever agenda she has with a lady in a green raincoat–Mike's mom. Every summer, Mike's parents have invited the whole gang from Camp Clearwater to their restaurant, Smokin' Elliot's BBQ Shack, for an end-of-summer celebration. Mike's mom nods to whatever Raina is telling her, hugging herself around the middle. Mike's dad stands beside her. They look like the two most tired people on earth. I guess they probably haven't slept much these past six days.

My throat feels dry. I swallow. I knew it would be like this. I've seen candlelight vigils on TV and in movies. They are sad events. I *knew* this would be sad. But now that I'm here, the reality of it begins to weigh on me. It's heavy. It's suffocating. I close my eyes and breathe in the smell of the Starling, waiting for the swelling in my throat to subside.

"Hey, Nate." I turn around and am relieved to see Mr. Evans. He smiles warmly and holds up his burning candle to light my wick. "How are ya, kiddo?"

"All right," I lie. "How are you doing, Mr. Evans?"

He sighs and looks toward the water. "Oh, you know."

I guess. None of us is doing great.

He looks back, and his warm smile returns as Mercy and Owen appear beside me. "Hey, guys."

Owen nods.

"Hi, Mr. Evans," says Mercy a little too brightly considering the occasion. She winces when she realizes her mistake. Mercy can't help being Mercy.

Mr. Evans doesn't seem to mind. "Thanks for making the trip, kids."

"Are you kidding?" says Mercy. "It's not like we could just sulk at home. I mean, it's *Mike* we're talking about."

There's a long, silent pause, and Owen glares at Mercy.

"It's Mike," I agree.

Mr. Evans doesn't seem to be listening anyway. He's watching the road, where all the cars are parked. He looks different. Like another person. His mouth is tight in a grim line, his forehead creased in the middle. Not like the Mr. Evans I've grown up with. What's happened to Mike has changed him. I guess it's changed all of us.

"Evans!" A man wearing a tan leather coat climbs out of a silver pickup and waves in our direction. "Hey, Evans!" His voice is loud, gruff, like the noisy muffler on his truck. Heads turn toward the commotion.

Mr. Evans pats my shoulder. "Excuse me, kids." He leaves us to join his friend as speakers spit and crackle to life. Mike's mom stands by the water's edge, holding a microphone.

"Hello?" she says to the crowd. Everyone falls quiet. She clutches the microphone close to her chin and wipes at her left eye. "Thank–thank you for being here. Thank you for coming out tonight for Michael. It's been six days–" She stops, and we can hear her shaky breathing through the speakers.

Raina appears beside her, placing a hand on her shoulder and whispering something in her ear. Mike's mom nods, gathering her strength, and speaks into the mic again. "It's been six days since my son first went missing on the Starling River..."

Chapter Three

Michael Elliot went missing on the Starling River six days ago. His kayak was found by Search and Rescue. It was caught in a whirlpool in the part of the river known as the Black Hole. No one knows why he went out on his own. No one knows why he didn't tell anyone he was going. And now no one knows if he'll ever come back.

The waters of the Starling aren't very forgiving. No one knows that better than I do.

But if the Starling ever loved a person, that person is Mike Elliot. It wouldn't swallow *him* up. Not his river.

I'm in one of the counselor cabins, sitting on Mike's bunk. The wall beside it is plastered with photos of summers past, Mike smiling out from every one of them. Pictures of Mike on the river, sitting around campfires, arms around other Clearwater campers. There are even a few pictures of me here, standing with Mike, the two of us in PFDs and helmets. Mike is grinning his bright white smile, and I'm staring up at him like he's some kind of superhero. I guess I always sort of thought he was.

Oh, Mike. What happened to you?

The vigil ended an hour ago. People said a few nice things about Mike, about what a great person he is, about what a fighter he is. How strong he is. His dad asked that we all not lose hope. That we pray for Mike to be found safe and sound. People cried.

I didn't cry. Because I couldn't understand it. Even now, looking at his picture, I can't figure out what happened. Mike taught me everything I know about river kayaking. Taught me how to be safe on the water, how to respect the river. Why would he just take off on his own and not tell anyone? It doesn't make any sense.

"What are you doing in here?"

I jump, slamming my head into the bed above me.

"Whoa!" Raina runs over, placing her hand on my head where I bumped it. "Sorry, Nate. I didn't mean to scare you."

"I'm okay," I say, brushing her off.

She sighs and sits in the chair at Mike's desk. Her eyes roam over the pictures. "Hard to believe, isn't it?"

I nod.

She shakes her head and rubs her neck. "I just talked to him last week," she says. "He was sitting right where you are."

My back stiffens, and the bed is suddenly electric. I feel like I'm trespassing. "He was here already? But camp doesn't start for a couple weeks."

"All the counselors come up early. Mike earlier than most. Gives us time to plan activities, plan day trips and stuff. Mike couldn't wait for this year to start."

My hands cling to the quilted bedcover. He sent me an email a couple weeks ago saying how excited he was for me to take on the Nebula. I was excited too. Because I knew he was going to get me through it.

My eyes wander back over the pictures and along his desk. The cupboard behind Raina is filled with clothes–Mike's clothes. He'd already moved in for the summer.

"You're not going all the way back to the city tonight, are you?" Raina asks.

"No, Mr. Evans opened up the green-shirt cabins for us."

Raina nods. "You want me to walk you back?"

I shake my head.

"Sure?"

"I can find my way," I say.

She bites her lip and looks over at the pictures. I can tell she doesn't want to leave me on my own, but she nods and stands up, squeezing my arm before she leaves.

I stare at the picture of Mike and me in matching life vests and helmets. *What happened, Mike? Why would you go out there by yourself?* A lump begins to swell in my throat, and I have to look away. It's not like Mike to do something so reckless. So dangerous. Only an idiot would try to take on the Black Hole alone.

The memory of the white, frothing, furious water washes over my mind, and my stomach surges so that I feel like I'm going to be sick.

Mike is no idiot.

I notice a black case on the far edge of the desk. It's Mike's river knife.

I snap it up like it's going to run away on me. Mike's river knife is *here*. He went out on the Starling and left his river knife behind?

I pull it out of the sheath, staring at the glinting blade.

Brings me luck, his voice echoes in my mind.

Mike would *never* leave his knife behind.

My heart hammers in my chest. The *thud, thud, thud* of my blood pumps behind my ears.

Mike went out onto the Starling six nights ago, but he hadn't planned on it.

I sheath the knife and tuck it into my pocket. Then I race out of the cabin and sprint toward the green shirts' campsite.

Mercy and Owen are sitting on the porch of one of the cabins. "Where'd you go?" Mercy asks when she sees me.

"Nate," says Owen, getting to his feet, "are you okay?"

I pull the knife from my pocket and hold it out.

"What's that?" Mercy asks.

"Mike's river knife," I say, panting.

"What?" Owen's eyes go wide. "Where'd you get that?"

"It was in his cabin. He left it behind."

"Nate," says Mercy, "you stole Mike's river knife?"

"No! Don't you get it?" I yell. "Mike would never go anywhere without this thing!

He would have never gone out on the river if he didn't have his knife with him."

Mercy and Owen look at me like I've lost my mind. But I haven't. I'm finally starting to understand.

"Something made Mike head out onto the Starling that day," I tell them. "Something unexpected. And I bet that something chased him into the Black Hole."

Owen looks worried, his eyes darting to Mercy. She stares at the knife in my hand. "Like what, Nate?"

I have no idea.

But I'm going to find out.

Even if I have to face the Starling's worst waters again—for Mike, I will.

Chapter Four

It's late. The kind of late that's more accurately early. It's dark, but I can hear the chirping of birds. Dawn isn't far away. I haven't slept a wink. I lie on my back, staring at the slats in the bunk above me. Owen rustles overhead. He hasn't slept either. There's a crinkling to my left as Mercy wraps up the bag of crackers she's been munching. Raina let her stay in our cabin because camp hasn't officially started yet. None of us has slept. We've been racking our brains, trying to figure out what could have forced Mike into the Starling unexpectedly.

"What about Sarah Bauer?" Mercy says, her voice filling the silence.

Sarah Bauer. Last year she got to go to Argentina for the World Freestyle Kayak Championships. If there was anyone at Camp Clearwater better at riding the Starling than Mike, it was Sarah. A counselor like Mike, Sarah had been coming to Camp Clearwater for many years and was on a mission to compete in the Olympics. No one doubts she'll do it. Sarah and Mike were always trying to one up each other. Their competitiveness drove Mr. Evans crazy because it usually resulted in one or both of them pulling some stupid stunt that Mr. Evans considered a bad example to the rest of us. But Sarah Bauer seemed to always need to prove how much better than Mike she was. And Mike hated to lose.

I turn my head, and Mercy is up on one elbow, sleeping bag pulled up to her ears, cheeks stuffed with crackers.

"What about her?" Owen asks.

"Remember two summers ago?" she says. "When Sarah challenged Mike to that insanely stupid midnight run of the Nebula?"

I did remember. Mercy had tapped on the window of our cabin. She was outside with a few other girls. It was way after lights out, and being out of bed meant big trouble. But Sarah had challenged Mike to take on the Nebula in the dark, and word was Mike had accepted the challenge. And since Mercy and a bunch of the girls were already out of bed, I figured they wouldn't suspend all of us. So we went down to the Starling, ten of us in all.

Sarah and Mike were getting their boats ready. It was dangerous. It was stupid. We all knew that. But when Mike had expressed concern, Sarah accused him of being too scared. Mike couldn't have that. They would have both gone through with it, too, if Andrew Chin hadn't set off that flare to start the race. He had stolen it from the equipment shed on the beach, thinking it would be a pretty cool way to kick the whole thing off, like a gunshot. Real professional. What none of us counted on was how bright it would be. Mr. Evans saw the light and caught all of us just as Sarah and Mike were about to shove off. Everyone scattered as soon as they saw Mr. Evans's flashlight, but Mike and Sarah were knee-deep in the Starling and couldn't take off as quickly.

Mr. Evans was furious. Mike said later that he thought Mr. Evans's skin was going to peel right off his face from the way it strained while he yelled at them. Mike also said that Mr. Evans wanted to suspend the counselors, but instead he put them on LDU duty for the rest of the summer. That might not sound so bad, but trust me, no one wants LDU duty. Liquid Disposal Unit. All the soggy, soiled, juicy waste from mealtime has to go somewhere, like dishwater and salad dressing and melted ice cream and pickle juice and old spaghetti sauce. It all gets dropped over a mesh cloth over a grate. LDU duty is having to deal with all the grossest food bits left once the liquid has drained out. Mike hated Sarah for it.

"Did anybody see Sarah tonight?" Mercy asks.

I think back to the vigil, to the weeping faces in the crowd. None of them belonged to Sarah Bauer. "I didn't see her."

"Me neither," agrees Owen.

"That's weird, right?" Mercy sits cross-legged on her bunk. "I mean, she and Mike have been coming to Clearwater since what? Birth? And she can't even turn up to show a bit of support for a guy she's known almost her whole life?"

"They weren't exactly friends, Mercy," Owen points out.

"It's just common decency though, isn't it? I mean, even if you didn't like the guy, it's just the right thing to do. Why wouldn't she come?"

"Maybe she couldn't," I say. "Exams or something, I don't know." Sarah Bauer may be a vicious competitor, but I don't think she's a psychopath.

Mercy waves a hand. "Exams? Please. Like she couldn't get an extension for something like this. I'm checking her social media."

"And what exactly are you looking for?" asks Owen as Mercy takes out her phone. "It's not like her status is going to say *totally tricked Mike into getting lost on the Starling!*"

"I know that, dumb-dumb," she says, the light from her phone casting her face in a ghostly white light. "But maybe it'll say why she isn't here now."

"I don't know," says Owen. "I know she pushed Mike's buttons and all, but she's still a good person. I had her when I was a green shirt, and she was cool."

I was in Owen's cabin when we were green shirts, and Sarah took us on a day trip to Eagle Falls. I have to agree with him. She was all right, as long as Mike wasn't around. I couldn't imagine she'd do anything to hurt someone.

"What the...?" whispers Mercy.

I sit up. “What is it?”

She turns her screen so I can see–a picture of Sarah in her kayaking gear, smiling for a selfie with another smiling face. Mike’s.

“What’s Mike doing on the river with Sarah?” asks Mercy.

I take the phone from her and stare at the picture. Since when are Mike and Sarah friends? I look at the date at the bottom.

“It says the photo was added two weeks ago,” I say. “That’s, like, a week before Mike went missing.”

“See?” says Mercy. “I told you Sarah had something to do with it.”

Owen leans so far over the edge of his bunk to look at the phone that he nearly falls out.

“That doesn’t mean anything,” he says. “Look at them. They’re smiling.”

“Exactly! When have you ever seen those two smiling together?” says Mercy. “And now suddenly here they are together a week before Mike goes missing? And look what’s in the background.”

Behind Sarah and Mike is the unmistakable face of Witch Rock, just upriver from where they snapped the photo.

"This picture was taken on the Starling," says Mercy. "Sarah Bauer is from Clarenville. What's she doing coming all the way to Guilford Falls to hang out with a guy she hates?"

Owen doesn't say anything. He doesn't know how to answer those questions. None of us do. Only Sarah Bauer does.

I hand Mercy back her phone. "I say we go ask her."

Chapter Five

My fingernails are ready to rip off as I dig them under the windowsill of Mr. Evans's office. The frame is old and flaking, the wood rotting from too many damp Camp Clearwater mornings. My feet are itchy as the cold dew dries on my sandaled feet. I am standing on Owen's back, trying to balance.

"This is a really bad idea, Nate," Owen whispers, and I nearly fall.

"Keep still," I growl. "You're going to send me flying."

"Oh, I'm sorry. Am I not being a good enough footstool for you?"

He's being sarcastic, but no, he's not. Finally I manage to get the window up, and I'm faced with the screen.

"I was against this plan from the start," Owen grumbles. "If you don't like what I'm doing, then you should have had Mercy help you."

"Mercy has to bring the car around, Owen."

He doesn't say anything to that. He knows exactly why he's the one boosting me up instead of Mercy, but I guess he wants to make sure I know he's not happy about it.

I work my fingers along the screen's edge until it pops loose and falls into the dusty office.

"I'm in!" I say.

"Great," Owen mutters under my weight. "Now hurry, before we get caught."

I hoist myself up so that my stomach rests on the window ledge and then fall forward, toppling head over feet onto the floor of the office with a grunt.

"You okay?" Owen whispers from outside.

"Fine." I dust off my knees. My elbow burns with pain. A clock on the wall above the door reads *7:45 AM*. Mr. Evans usually doesn't come in until eight forty-five. That gives me plenty of time to look for Sarah's address.

I head over to the desk and pull open the drawers one by one. There are binders of camp itineraries and staff schedules–each counselor's name is written in a different color of ink. Mike's name appears in green on different days of the week. I feel a lump form in my throat. He was scheduled to be here today. I move on quickly, rifling through the mail bins behind the desk–letters from parents, permission forms and donation checks from local businesses like Higgins Autobody.

"Nate," Owen whispers. "I saw Raina over by the flagpole. Hurry up!"

If Raina is here, then Mr. Evans could show up any minute. I have to move faster. I notice a gray filing cabinet in the corner. I pull open the first drawer–jackpot.

The files are all color-coded, camper names printed neatly on white stickers. I thumb through them, looking for Sarah Bauer, but another name catches my eye—Nathan Andersen.

Me.

I open the file just a crack and peek inside. Permission forms and invoices from over the years. At the very back of the file is an orange piece of paper that looks like a report card. It's dated from my first year at Camp Clearwater. The heading reads *Progress Report*. At the top is a bunch of scribbly writing from Mr. Evans. *Mother informs us Nathan was traumatized last year when the current carried the paddle-boat he was in away from their cottage dock. Nathan nearly drowned when the boat capsized in the Black Hole. Park rangers pulled him from the river, and he spent three days in hospital. Skittish around water. Be encouraging. Don't push.*

I swallow, my lungs aching as the memory of the white water fills my mind. The river threw me, threw the boat, and I fell into the water. I remember it so vividly, the way the Starling swallowed me up. No, not the Starling. The Starling and I have become friends over the years. It's just that one part of the river, where the Starling becomes something else, something monstrous–where it becomes the Black Hole. That's what swallowed me up. What swallowed up Mike.

Mike.

His handwriting appears beneath Mr. Evans's notes in a different color of ink, the letters jagged and messy.

Nate's been awesome to work with. His progress has been inspirational to me personally. His courage and willingness to face his fears has taught me to challenge myself more, not just on the river, but also in my life outside Camp Clearwater. I really hope to see him back next year.

"Nate!" Owen whispers. "Nate!"

I've never seen this before. I remember how Mike helped me that first year–how he reintroduced me to the Starling. *His* Starling. A friendly, exciting place that made me forget the monster that had tried to kill me. Mike had been my hero. My eyes begin to burn as I read again the words he wrote.

"Nate!"

I glance over at the window just as I hear the sounds–keys jingling and a deep voice mumbling. Mr. Evans.

Quickly and quietly I place my file back in the drawer and close the cabinet.

Hide. I have to hide.

Over by the door I spot a stack of paddles and life jackets. I hurry across the room, crouch down and tuck myself in behind them.

The door opens.

"This is the third time you've called me, Bob," says Mr. Evans, walking across the floor. My eyes fall on the window screen on the floor. I hold my breath as he steps over it, not even noticing it. "I don't have anything new to tell you." Mr. Evans sits at his desk and removes his baseball cap.

The paddle in front of my face tips forward, and my hand shoots out, grabbing it before it can fall. I close my eyes, trying to calm my pounding pulse. I don't know what Mr. Evans would do if he found me in here. But it wouldn't be good. I know that much.

"I don't really see how that's relevant to our business, Bob." Mr. Evans sounds grumpy. He's never in a good mood before his coffee.

The door opens again, and Raina pops her head in. "Steve? Mr. and Mrs. Elliot are going to be here at ten for Mike's things."

Mr. Evans nods. Waves a hand for her to leave.

Raina doesn't move. "I think it's important that you meet them at the gate, don't you?"

He frowns and holds his hand over the phone. "Raina, I said yes, okay? I know. I'll be there."

"All right, all right," she says, closing the door as she goes. But goes where is the question. If she's out on the porch, I can't sneak away without her knowing I was in here. But I don't know how I can get out the door as long as Mr. Evans is here. I'm stuck until he leaves.

"Yeah, Bob," says Mr. Evans. "No, they haven't found Mike Elliot yet...No, it doesn't look good."

His voice is quiet, grim, and I feel the room getting smaller.

"Of course we're still searching. What else can we do?" He sighs. "Well, we're not giving up hope, if that's what you're implying. And to be honest, Bob, I don't feel very comfortable discussing it with you."

I nod to myself. We're not giving up hope. Not me, not Mercy and Owen, and not Mr. Evans, from the sounds of it. I'm glad to know we're not alone in our mission to bring Mike home.

"Since when are you so interested, Bob?" asks Mr. Evans. "What are you...?" Mr. Evans suddenly jumps up from his seat. I cringe, sure he's spotted me. But no, it's the screen on the floor. "No, I don't...yeah, I understand." His voice has changed. It's almost a whisper as he stares up at the open window. "I understand, Bob. I won't."

He pulls the phone away from his ear and stands there at his desk, his knuckles rapping the wood. He's facing my direction. Can he see me? No. He's looking at nothing. His eyes are unfocused. Whatever he's thinking about, it's enough to keep him from noticing me.

He pulls open the drawer in front of him, pulls out a piece of paper and carefully folds it, then stuffs it into his pocket.

Finally, he heads for the door.

The slam of the door knocks another paddle loose. It crashes onto the floor. I wait for Mr. Evans to come back in. But I hear his footsteps getting more and more faint. I'm alone again.

But there's no time to lose.

I run over to the cabinet and flip through the files, rifling through the *B*s. She's right at the front. *Bauer, Sarah.*

I grab the whole folder and head for the door.

"Nate?" Owen. He's still at the window. "You all right, man?"

"Yeah," I say. "I got it."

Chapter Six

2247 Oak Tree Lane.

We stand on the porch of Sarah Bauer's house. It's white with blue shutters and flowers in the window boxes. A nice place. Warm and inviting. But I'm not here to relax. I need facts. Answers. And if Sarah Bauer has any of them, then I need to speak with her.

"Maybe no one's home," says Owen, a little too hopefully.

Mercy nudges me with her elbow. "Knock again, Nate."

I knock, and the three of us wait, but there's no answer.

Just then a black van pulls into the driveway. A woman in a nurse's uniform hops out, holding a bag of groceries. "Can I help you?"

"We're looking for Sarah," says Mercy.

The woman squints at us before glancing up at the second floor. "I'm her mom. Sarah's not feeling well," she says. "You kids might not have heard, but she lost a friend of hers–"

"He's not dead." The words fall out of my mouth on their own, and everyone stares at me.

"Oh god," Sarah's mom says. "They found him?"

I shake my head. "I just meant–" I start, but Mercy steps in front of me, changing the subject.

"We're from Camp Clearwater, ma'am. We're friends of Mike Elliot."

She nods sadly, making her way up the porch. She opens the door. "I can't guarantee she'll want to see you."

We follow her inside. The interior is bright and warm, like the outside. There are flowers on every table and shelf. The air smells like lavender.

"Sarah's been a wreck since she found out," says Mrs. Bauer. "She hasn't really even left her room much. So I don't imagine she's up for visitors."

"We understand," says Owen kindly.

Mercy glares at him. As far as Mercy is concerned, this is an investigation. And there's no room for kindness in a serious investigation.

Sarah's mom puts the bag of groceries on the counter and heads for the stairs. "I'll just go let her know."

The three of us stand silently, listening to the footfalls upstairs. We can hear the murmurs of two people talking.

"Do you think she'll want to see us?" Owen whispers.

"If she doesn't," says Mercy, "then we'll know it's because she's hiding something."

"And how exactly does it mean that?" asks Owen.

Mercy rolls her eyes. "Why else would she refuse to see us after we drove all this way?"

"Guys!" I hiss. "Be quiet."

I hear the floorboards on the stairs creaking. Sarah comes around the corner. She's in pajamas, her hair up in a messy ponytail. Her nose is red, and there are dark circles under her eyes. "Nate Andersen," she says, surprised.

"Hi, Sarah."

"What are you guys doing here?"

Mercy and Owen look nervously at me, not sure how to answer. I don't really know how either.

"Can we talk?" I ask her.

"What about?"

"Mike."

Her chin quivers, and she looks away.

"Sarah?" her mom calls from upstairs.

"It's fine, Mom," she says. "I'm fine." She walks toward the front door, holding it open for the three of us. "Let's talk then."

We all shuffle out onto the porch. Sarah takes a seat on the top step.

"So," she says, folding her knees up to her chest, "you drove all the way here to talk to me about Mike?"

I take a seat beside her. "We did."

She nods, her finger chipping at some white paint peeling off the step. "How was the vigil?"

"It was all right, I guess. Lots of people turned out."

"We noticed you weren't there," says Mercy. I shoot her a look. Mercy doesn't do subtle.

"I just, uh..." Sarah trails off, dabbing her eye on her sleeve. "I just couldn't be there, you know?"

"No, we don't know."

"Mercy," I warn.

"No, seriously," Mercy says, ignoring me, "we all went there to show our support. Why didn't you?"

"What is her problem?" Sarah asks.

"We saw your post online, Sarah." Mercy holds out her phone, the selfie of Sarah and Mike at Witch Rock, blown up on the screen. "If you guys were such besties, why couldn't you show up for his vigil?"

Sarah doesn't answer. As she stares at the picture, her eyes well up.

"I mean, what kind of friend are you that you wouldn't make the drive out?"

"Mike is not my friend," Sarah snaps, tears falling from her eyes. "He's my boyfriend, okay?"

"Your *boyfriend*?" I am shocked. The way they acted around each other, I never would have thought they could like each other that way.

Sarah points at Mercy's phone. "That was our nine-month anniversary. We went out on the Starling together. He planned a picnic for us at Witch Rock." She glares at Mercy in that way only Sarah Bauer can. "That's why I couldn't go to the vigil, all right? It was too much, too real. It was like if I went, then I'd be admitting he was gone."

Mercy takes a step back and puts her phone down. I can see she's regretting coming at Sarah so hard.

"Sarah?" I say. "Did anything happen when you guys went out on the Starling? Did Mike say anything or–"

"What?" Sarah snaps. "You're a detective now? I've been over everything with the sheriff from Guilford Falls already."

"What did you tell the sheriff?"

"We hit the Starling–it was good water."

"Did you tell anyone you were going?" I ask.

She rolls her eyes. "We're not newbs, Nate. Yes, we checked in at the ranger station. Launched from Shoal Point, hit the Kessel Run and the Milky Way on our way to Witch Rock."

"The Milky Way?" Mr. Evans takes the second-years down the Milky Way as a beginner lesson in the kayaks. Class One. It's basically a big Jacuzzi. And as for the Kessel Run, Raina and Sarah take the first-years in the big rafts for their first taste of white water. It's barely a step up from the Milky Way. Pretty tame waters for paddlers as good as Sarah and Mike.

"That's how you get to Witch Rock, Nate." Sarah glares at me. I don't mean to sound suspicious. I just want to understand what happened to Mike. "We were going to hit the Nebula after our picnic."

The Nebula. Class Four. That's more like it for Sarah and Mike. And beyond the Nebula...

"Did Mike say anything about trying the Black Hole?" I ask her.

She looks away, swallows. "No...but I did."

Mercy looks to me, her eyes going wide. I am sure she's thinking what I'm thinking, that maybe that's why Mike took on the Black Hole alone. To impress Sarah.

"What did Mike say?" I ask.

"What do you think he said?" Sarah snaps again. "No, obviously. It was a stupid idea. And he set me straight."

That sounded like Mike. But still, he had done it. He'd taken on the Black Hole not two weeks after Sarah suggested it. Did she tease him for not wanting to try it?

Did it eat at him until he just had to try to prove to her that he wasn't afraid? No. Mike wouldn't be that stupid.

"Besides," Sarah continues, "by the time we were done the Nebula, it was nearly sundown. There wouldn't have been time for the Black Hole anyway, thanks to his obsession with the environment."

"What do you mean?"

She sighs, rubbing her knees. "After the Milky Way he spotted some swamp grossness onshore and climbed out to take a look. I told him to leave it, but he was all *This is Camp Clearwater property* and had to investigate."

"What do you mean, *swamp grossness*?"

"I don't know," Sarah says. "It looked like swampy pools of green from the shoreline. It was stupid. Just pond scum, you know? But he made us spend, like, an hour there while he took pictures. Ate up our entire morning."

"Did you tell the sheriff about that?"

"What?"

"The pond scum."

Sarah looks confused. "No, why would I?"

"But it was on Camp Clearwater property?"

She shrugs. "I think so. I mean, I don't know. Not any part of the grounds I've been to. But Mike said it was. It was just north of camp. Why, what are you thinking? Do you think I should have told the sheriff about it?"

I don't know.

Maybe this pond scum is more than nothing.

Chapter Seven

We leave Sarah's and get back on the road to Guilford Falls in Mercy's old car. Before we go, I promise Sarah I'll let her know if we find out anything else. Her mom gives us a container full of homemade blueberry muffins.

I sit in the back seat, the wind from Mercy's open window whipping my hair. I think about what Sarah told us.

"What are you thinking?" Owen asks from the passenger seat, one cheek stuffed with muffin.

"I think I want to see this pond scum for myself."

"Why?" asks Mercy. "What do you think it has to do with anything?"

"I don't know," I admit. "Sarah said it was north of camp. The Nebula is north, and so is the Black Hole. Maybe Mike went back to check it out by himself. Maybe he got lost somehow or maybe...I don't know. Maybe the water level was too high, and he lost control. Maybe someone scared him. I don't know! But that's the point, isn't it? We don't know what happened. All we can do is look for clues. Maybe this is one."

Owen and Mercy exchange glances but don't say anything. I know they think I'm crazy. But I don't hear them coming up with any better ideas.

"And what if," Mercy says, slowly, carefully, "we don't find any answers with this pond-scum business?"

Then we're at a dead end.

I'm quiet, not wanting to say what I'm thinking. But I know that they are thinking it too.

We drive in silence, and I stare out the window, watching the pine and birch whip by.

WHAP!

Owen and I nearly fall over as Mercy swerves the car. There's a growl under the wheels as we skid on the gravel. Mercy brings us to a stop at the side of the road.

"What was that?" Owen gasps.

"A rock," says Mercy. "Oh man, my windshield."

There's a crack spidering out from the middle of the windshield. It's a big crack, obscuring some of the view.

"I'm going to have to get a new windshield!"

"How much will that cost?"

"I don't know, Owen!" she snaps. "Probably a lot!" She takes out her phone and starts to type.

"What are you doing?" I ask.

"Trying to figure out where to go to get my windshield fixed."

Owen is way ahead of her. "There's a place just outside downtown Guilford Falls.

Higgins Autobody. The map says it's about six miles."

The body shop looks run-down. The metal fence is rusted and falling down in places, and junk parts are strewn everywhere around the property. But the garage itself looks busy. Several men are working on various cars. Owen and I wait against the wall, watching customers come and go. Most of them look annoyed.

A shiny silver pickup comes tearing into the lot, the roar from its muffler drowning out all the sounds of the shop. It drives up to the office door, and for a second I think it's going to punch straight through the wall. But the driver slams on the brakes at the last second. I realize I've seen the truck before. At the vigil.

A big man steps out wearing a tan leather jacket–Mr. Evans's friend. He looks furious. He slams the door of the truck. The license plate says *Higgins*. I guess this is his shop. He whips open the door to the office. "Eddie!" he booms.

Mercy comes back to the car. She has been talking to one of the mechanics. "He says it'll take a few hours," she tells us.

"What are we supposed to do for a few hours?" Owen asks.

Mercy shrugs. "It's about a fifteen-minute walk into town. Maybe we could get ice cream or something at Smokin' Elliot's?"

"Great idea!" says Owen.

But I am not interested. I don't feel like sitting around eating ice cream while Mike is still missing.

"You guys go ahead," I tell them. "I'm going to try to check out the pond scum."

"What?" says Mercy. "Sarah said it was close to camp."

"Yeah?"

"Nate," says Owen, "that's, like, a half-hour drive. It'll take you hours to walk there."

I shrug. "It'll take hours for the car to be ready."

"You don't even know exactly where it is."

"That's why I need to start looking." I am not changing my mind.

Nate and Mercy exchange glances again.

"We'll come with you," says Mercy.

I shake my head. "You have to stick around for the car. Thanks, but I'll be fine, guys. I have my phone."

"Fine," Mercy says finally. "Text us when you get there. Let us know exactly where you are, and we can pick you up."

"Cool," I agree. "Text you later."

With that, I make my way toward the main road to camp. After a few minutes I glance back and see that Mercy and Owen have started making their way into town. *Great! Now I'm free to follow the Starling.* I double back, toward the riverbank. I know Mercy and Owen wouldn't like this plan, me walking alone in the woods, but it will be faster. Following the river toward camp will take me half the amount of time that taking the road would. And besides, Mike saw the pools of pond scum from the Starling, not the road. It will be easier for me to find them this way.

I hope.

Chapter Eight

I check my phone. No messages from Owen or Mercy. That's probably because I have no service. I've been walking along the Starling for two and a half hours now. And I haven't found anything. Camp Clearwater can't be too much farther. If I don't find it soon, I'll have to head back to the road and call Owen and Mercy. Otherwise, they're likely to send the park rangers out to find me.

Just as I'm thinking about heading for the road, I spot the beach of Camp

Clearwater. Kayaks are neatly lined along the edge. *Just a little farther.*

I make my way along the camp's shore. I don't see a soul. Not Mr. Evans or Raina or anyone. The camp is deserted. I'm glad. I really don't want to have to answer any questions about why I'm out here on my own.

The clear shores of Camp Clearwater begin to give way to shrub and bramble. Thorns and sticks poke at my feet as I move beyond the camp's boundaries. The pools should be around here somewhere.

I walk along the shore, my eyes turned from the water, peering through the trees. There's nothing but forest as far as the eye can see.

And then I spot it. A glint of sunlight off a reflective surface between the trees.

I step away from the river and into the shade of the pines. There's a smell. Like rotten eggs and hot glue. As I get closer, I can see that it's not just one but four pond-sized pools of murky water. An electric-green algae grows in clumps on the surfaces.

This is it. Mike was standing right here, right where I am. There's a hum of excitement in my skin, like I can feel Mike close by.

"I'm comin' for you, man," I say. And for the first time, I really feel like it's true.

I take out my phone and begin to snap pictures. I don't know what else to do but exactly what Mike did. I wander around the pools, kicking at the ground, looking for signs of him. There's nothing. I glance from the pools to the waters of the Starling not far away. If he came back by kayak to check out the pools, then why didn't he just head back to camp when he was done? Why go down to the Nebula and then the Black Hole, of all things?

To my left I see a couple empty barrels. Green-and-black steel drums with orange, foamy gunk crusted at their bases. And a symbol in a yellow triangle on each of them. It's faded and covered in grime, but I still recognize it. A skull and crossbones. Toxic.

What is all this doing here? And so close to Camp Clearwater?

A sound hums in the distance–a boat. It's getting closer.

Through the trees I spot a fishing boat making its way down the Starling, the nose pointed toward the bank. It's headed straight toward me.

I duck behind the barrels as the boat grinds onto the shore. Two men–a big fat dude with a round nose and overalls missing one strap, and a shorter man with long red hair in a ponytail and a beard like a pirate's. They hop out of the boat and wrestle with more of the same steel drums, struggling to lift them out of the boat. Each one rolls a barrel toward the edge of the nearest pool, then goes back for another. Four barrels.

The big one takes a sniff of the still water and spits. "We're going to need to dig another pool soon."

The bearded guy says nothing, focused on pouring the contents of his barrel.

"Ed!" the big one snaps. "Did you hear me?"

"Yeah, Dale," the bearded guy says.

"Tell you one thing," Dale continues. "The boss is going to have to start paying me a lot more for this kind of work."

Ed still doesn't say anything, just gets to work dumping another barrel.

"Especially if he expects us to keep our mouths shut about that camp kid."

My heart stops. Mike.

"Going to talk, are you?" asks Ed, finally looking up from his work.

"If I don't get more money? You're darn right."

Ed smirks and shakes his head.

"You don't believe me?" asks Dale.

"Nope."

"That right?"

"Yeah, that's right," says Ed. "Cuz if you talk, you're going to have to explain how you chased the kid into the river, and since Bob wasn't here when it happened, who do you think the police are going to blame?"

"Hey, genius," says Dale, grabbing a hold of the barrel, "I chased the kid back to that camp they all go to. As I recall, it was *you* who made him take the kayak in the water."

"Me?"

"You took off after him in the boat!"

"On your orders."

"Still," says Dale, "not much I could do standing on the shore, was there? He ended up in that white water because of you. Not me."

The two men glare at each other, and I imagine Mike running along the shore, that big goon chasing after him. He probably thought the kayak was his best chance to get away–until Ed came after him in the fishing boat. I knew it. Mike didn't go into the Black Hole because he wanted to. He did it because he was trying to avoid getting caught by these guys. He did it because he *had* to.

I lift my phone. I want a picture of their faces. I want to give the sheriff whatever she needs to find these guys. Quietly I press the button, and when I check the screen, there's a branch blocking the view of them. *Darn it*. I need to get closer.

I wait, frozen, for the right moment. I want them to be focused on what they're doing so they don't look up and spot me for the two seconds I need to step free of the barrel and snap a picture.

Who are these guys, anyway? I've got two names, Ed and Dale. But what good is that? What are they doing out here, dumping this stuff? What is all this? Illegal, whatever it is. Illegal enough to risk getting Mike killed so they don't get caught. I need to be careful. I don't know what they'll do if they find me, but I know it won't be good.

The big one lets out an angry "Bah!" and starts heading back to the boat. As he passes me, I manage to take a picture without him noticing. I look at my screen. It's a great shot. Clear. There's no denying his face. Now I just need one of Ed.

Ed starts wheeling an empty barrel. Now's my chance. I crawl out from my hiding spot and wait for Ed to stop moving. He leaves the barrel by a stump and takes off his hat, wiping his forehead. *Snap.*

"Hey!"

Behind me, Dale stands up in the boat. He points directly at me.

"Ed! There's another one!"

Ed spots me, and my stomach leaps into my throat.

Run.

I tear off into the trees, the men shouting behind me.

Mike, my brain whispers. They chased Mike. And now he's missing.

And now they're after me.

Chapter Nine

I sprint into the trees, hoping the branches of the pines will hide me. But Ed isn't far behind. I glance back, and here he comes, hurdling logs and plowing through brush like a killer robot. I pump my legs as fast as they'll go. But another glance is enough to tell me Ed is faster than I am. I had a decent head start, but he's gaining on me.

Hide. I should hide. But it's no use. Ed is too close.

"Get your ass back here!" he roars.

I scramble under a fallen tree, hoping he's too big to follow. He is. But it doesn't matter. He leaps over it like an Olympian.

My heart pounds.

My lungs burst.

I can't keep this up much longer. He'll be on me any second.

And then I hear it. The roar of the Starling.

I race toward the water and stop just on the edge of the rocky shore. The water is white, boiling. Furious. The Nebula.

"End of the line, boy." I spin around to see Ed not five feet away, chest heaving as he gulps for breath. "There's nowhere left to run."

He's right. All he has to do is lunge and he can grab me.

I feel the mist of the rapids at my back.

There's nowhere left to run.

So I jump.

I'm swallowed up by frothing, bubbling white. It envelops me, pulls me down, and a panic–old and familiar–takes hold. The same panic I felt the first time I fell into white water. I remember the crushing weight. I remember the push and the pull. And I remember the fight.

In water this angry, you have to fight.

I kick for the surface, a ceiling of foam above me. I kick so hard, my legs are about to rip off.

And then I'm free, breaking the surface, air filling my lungs.

Ed stands on the shore, shouting. But he's not coming after me. Not into this torrent.

The water slams me down again and carries me away. It's fast. So fast. Like I'm nothing but a leaf.

I claw for the surface and break free again. I'm downstream. No Ed. Not sure where I am. I gasp for air, but another rush of water pounds me. It fills my lungs. And I'm under again.

I tug and pull and the panic swells inside of me.

How did I survive this before? The Starling is so powerful. So raging. How could anyone survive this?

The key is not to panic. Mike's voice is in my head. He taught us every year at Camp Clearwater what to do in an emergency. But I'm so frightened, so desperate for air, that I can't think.

My shoulder bashes into a rock, pain exploding, and I'm spinning, tumbling. My knee bashes riverbed. More searing pain.

I kick up from the bottom and burst free of the water, gulping in a breath.

Go with the flow, Nate, Mike says. *On your back. Use your legs to kick off obstacles in your way.*

I do like Mike has instructed me a thousand times before. I roll onto my back, keeping my feet out in front, and try to steer around rocks. But the world is whipping by so fast. And the water keeps pounding. *Inhale in the troughs. Hold your breath when the wave crests.*

And then I see the strainer–a massive log lying across the river. If I get pinned up against it, I'll be stuck. I'll drown.

Frantically I roll onto my stomach and try to avoid it, but there's no way. The water is too fast, and it's launching me right toward it.

So I swim directly at it. With everything in me, I paddle for the tree, letting the water rocket me forward. As I reach it, I use the momentum and vault myself over. My head falls back into the water, face first, and I'm flipped. Water fills my nose.

I break the surface again, gulping and trying to get onto my back again like Mike taught me.

The shore is closer now. The east bank. It's closer.

And the world is going by more slowly. The rapids are breaking up. I can get to the bank.

I roll onto my front and angle myself against the current, swimming for dry land.

I heave myself onto the bank, sputtering and gasping for breath. I lay there, trying to calm my racing heart.

I made it.

I survived the Nebula.

What would have happened if it had been the Black Hole?

Chapter Ten

Busted.

My phone is completely busted. It's sopping wet, the screen cracked. I have no way to call Owen and Mercy. And, worse than that, the pictures I risked my neck for are gone.

I sit in the mud on the banks of the Starling, water dripping down from my hair and into my eyes. My shoulder aches where I hit it, and my knee is bleeding, jeans torn. My clothes are soaked. My shoes are gone—the current ripped them off my feet.

I glance around at the forest beside me. It's dense brush. And no wonder. The east bank of the Starling is all part of a National Forest Reserve. No people. No roads. Just endless trees and swamp. I have to get back to civilization. Camp is half a day's walk back the way I came. I can be there before dark. True, I'm on the wrong side of the river. But it's calm water at camp. I can swim across.

I shudder. The idea of getting back in the water so soon is not something I want to do. But it's better than sitting here forever.

I drag my aching body to my feet and begin my long stumble back toward Camp Clearwater.

It's tough going. The ground is all roots and twigs and spiky things that poke and stab at my bare feet. It's enough pain to distract me from my aching shoulder. But my knee hasn't stopped bleeding, a steady stream of red trailing down my leg.

After about an hour I take a seat on a rock and inspect the wound. Pain radiates through me as I press around the gash. It's deep. The skin around it is pink and puffy. The inside is red, and I can see enough torn flesh to make me queasy.

Maybe I should try to wrap it. Keep pressure on it. But with what? I'm still soaked. And I feel like a wet bandage will do more harm than good.

I glance around hopelessly for something to use on my knee. The water is calmer here. Still fast, but the white water is well behind me.

A sound rises over the rush of the Starling.

A boat is coming.

A little tin fishing boat. Ed and Dale.

I scramble back to the trees and hide in the brush.

"For the last time, I'm not going in there!" I can see Dale sitting at the back of the boat, hand on the rudder. Voices carry easily over the water.

"You want to explain how we let this happen again?" shouts Ed from the bow.

"I want to be alive to do it, yeah! I'm not going in those rapids."

Ed says nothing, staring downstream. I edge a little farther back, making certain they can't see me.

"Kid's dead anyway," says Dale. "No one can swim through that."

"What if he climbed out onshore somewhere?"

"You said the same thing about the Elliot kid," says Dale.

My stomach clenches. These guys chased me into the river just like they did Mike.

"Come on," says Dale, "let's go."

The motor revs, and the boat turns back. I'm alone again with the Starling. They think the river killed me. But it didn't. The Starling is my home. It didn't kill me when I was little. It didn't kill me now.

It didn't kill me because Mike taught me how to survive it.

And if I can survive by doing what Mike taught me, I know he must have survived it too.

Chapter Eleven

"Are you sure about this, Nate?"

Mr. Evans watches me, wide-eyed, from behind his desk.

I'm sitting in his office. Raina is cleaning and bandaging the gash on my leg. When I made it back to Camp Clearwater, Raina saw me waving my arms on the opposite bank. She zipped across in the camp's motorboat and picked me up. Then she took me straight to see Mr. Evans.

"Do you think you could lead us back there?" Raina asks, looking up from my knee.

She's mad. She's been fuming since I told her everything that happened.

"I don't know if that's such a good idea," Mr. Evans says quickly. "If these guys are as dangerous as Nate says..."

"Well," huffs Raina, "I bet they're real tough guys when it's two against a *kid*. I'd like to see them try to pull that nonsense with us."

"They left anyway," I say. "I saw them take off in their boat."

"What color was the boat?" asks Raina.

I shrug. Gray, black, navy. I wasn't paying attention to the color.

"All right," says Raina, getting to her feet, "if we take my truck, do you think you could recognize this dump site from the road?"

I nod. The neon green of the algae will make the ponds unmistakable.

Raina heads for the door, and I stand up.

"Just hang on a second!" says Mr. Evans. He looks at me with concern. "Nate, you've been through a lot today. You don't have to do this if you don't want to."

He's right. I'm exhausted. My clothes are still damp. I have no shoes. But I *do* want to do this. "It's for Mike."

Raina nods approvingly. "Brave man, Nate."

But Mr. Evans doesn't look so sure. He bites his lip. I remember the words he wrote in my file–*skittish around water. Don't push.* He doesn't want to make me do something I'm not ready for. But I'm more than ready. I want Mike found. And getting these guys will help make that happen.

We all pile into Raina's truck–an old rusty pickup with a Camp Clearwater bumper sticker. The inside is clean and orderly, like Raina. It smells like cinnamon. The clock says six thirty. Owen and Mercy must be freaking out. With my phone dead, I haven't been able to text them. They haven't come back to Clearwater yet. So they must still be in town, waiting for Mercy's car.

We drive along the road, me sitting by the window. My nose is pressed to the glass.

I stare through the trees, keeping a careful eye out for the pools.

Finally I catch a flash of green.

"Stop!" I shout.

Raina slams on the breaks, and Mr. Evans nearly smashes his face on the dashboard.

"Do you see something, Nate?" asks Raina.

Through the pines, the unmistakable green sludge glints in the patches where the sun breaks through the branches. "That's the spot."

Raina turns the truck off the road, and we follow a dirt path into the forest. As we get closer, the other ponds come into view. Four in all.

We get out of the car. Raina and I make our way over to the ponds. She kicks at one of the empty barrels and swears.

"Industrial waste of some kind," she says. "Been at it for months, it looks like." She looks toward the Starling, flowing not far away. "This is definitely Clearwater property." She turns back to Mr. Evans. "Isn't it, Steve?"

Mr. Evans is leaning against the truck, kicking at the ground.

"What kind of jerk thinks they can just dump their poison out here and nobody will ever find out about it?" says Raina.

The kind like Ed and Dale.

Mr. Evans sighs–a long and heavy sound–and lets his head drop. Poor Mr. Evans. He looks so defeated, like somehow this is his fault. After all, it happened on his watch. If someone's abusing Clearwater property, it's Mr. Evans's job to put a stop to it. And Mike–would he still be missing if Mr. Evans had known about this sooner?

"It's not your fault, Mr. Evans." The words just tumble out. I don't want him to blame himself. Don't want him to beat himself up because of something Ed and Dale did.

He looks up, surprised. And he grins. "Thanks, Nate."

I nod. He still looks upset. I know he's going to keep blaming himself. But hopefully, now that we know about this we can find Mike faster, and he won't have to feel guilty much longer.

"Well," says Raina, "I guess the next step is to go report all this to Sheriff Nichols. I could take you, but I volunteered to cover the dinner shift at Smokin' Elliot's."

Mr. Evans pushes off from the truck. "I'll do it. You guys don't have to worry about it. I'll go report it."

"Don't you think Nate should be there?"

"I think he's been through enough, Raina."

"I don't mind," I say. "Really. I can describe these guys. And when we find Mike, he can back me up."

Mr. Evans and Raina exchange nervous glances.

"What?" I ask.

Raina folds her hands together like she's going to pray. "Nate–"

"Come on, Nate," Mr. Evans says quickly. "We'll go to town, you and me."

Raina smiles sadly and nods.

My stomach tightens. Whatever she was going to say, she's thought better of it. But it was something about Mike.

Maybe that she wants me to be ready for a bad outcome. Wants me to be realistic. But I am being realistic. This is Mike's river. If anyone can survive the Starling, it's Mike Elliot.

Chapter Twelve

I'm in the passenger's seat of Mr. Evans's van. We've both been quiet since we left Camp Clearwater. I can't stop thinking about Mike. About what could have happened to him. All so someone could dump toxic garbage without consequence. It makes me angry. So angry I could scream. I think of him alone in the woods somewhere. Scared. Alone. To try to think of something else, I focus on the music playing on the radio.

Mr. Evans hits the volume knob, and

the car is quiet. "You must be starving," he says. "It's well after dinnertime."

"I'm okay."

"What would your parents think if I let you waste away?"

I shrug. My parents had wanted to come with me to Mike's vigil. But I told them this was something I had to do with my friends from Clearwater. "I'm more worried about Owen and Mercy. I haven't texted them to let them know I'm okay."

"Where are they?" asks Mr. Evans.

"Downtown. They were going to get ice cream at Smokin' Elliot's last time I saw them."

Streetlights come into view, the dark of the forest giving way to the sparse lights of the town of Guilford Falls. It's such a little place, but compared to how deserted the land around Camp Clearwater is, this place is a metropolis.

"Why don't you go get dinner with them?" Mr. Evans says. "Get some pizza or something?"

I frown, confused. "But the sheriff–"

"I can talk to the sheriff." Mr. Evans pulls onto Main Street, his eyes on the road.

I shake my head. "You didn't see the guys. I have to do this. Only I can do this."

Mr. Evans sighs. "Nate, I appreciate that you want to be brave for Mike's sake. And you've proven you are brave. But you don't have to be a hero here."

His handwriting in my file scribbles across my mind–*don't push.* He's still worried I'm too fragile for this.

"I'm not afraid of these guys," I say.

"I didn't say you were. I'm just saying things aren't simple here." He pulls the car over to the side of the road. We're parked in front of Smokin' Elliot's BBQ Shack. Mike's family's restaurant. Mr. Evans turns to me, his face serious. "What happened to you today, what happened to Mike–this is getting dangerous. I think it would be good if I talked to the sheriff by myself first. We don't know if these guys are watching the station, waiting for you to turn up."

I hadn't considered that. And after the way they came after me, it makes sense that they would be on the lookout for me.

Mr. Evans sighs. "I'd just feel more comfortable going in there on my own and keeping you out of it for now. I'll tell Sheriff Nichols you can provide a description if she wants one. But she can get it from you at Clearwater."

I'm quiet. Mr. Evans is probably right.

He fishes into his pocket and pulls out a twenty-dollar bill. "Here," he says, handing it to me. "Get some dinner at the BBQ Shack with Owen and Mercy. You've done enough today. Just take it easy for tonight."

I shake my head, refusing the money. "I don't want to take it easy until Mike's found."

"Nate, that could be..." Mr. Evans's arms drop in his lap, and he looks away from me. He's frowning. Something's wrong.

"What?" I ask him.

"Nate..." He looks back at me. There's sadness in his eyes. "I didn't know how to tell you this earlier. Neither did Raina. But...they've called off the search."

My breath catches in my throat.

"They've exhausted all ground and air efforts to find him," Mr. Evans explains. "There's just nothing more they can do at this point."

I can't breathe. The ground falls away from me.

I claw at the door of the van. It's locked. I can't get out.

I need air.

I need to breathe.

"Hang on, hang on," says Mr. Evans, frantically reaching for the Unlock button.

With a *click* the doors unlock, and I pull the handle and tumble out of the van. The world is spinning. I stagger to the curb. There's a big planter of yellow flowers. I lean on it, trying to force air into my lungs.

Mr. Evans is beside me, rubbing my back. "I know, Nate. Just take a deep breath."

"Nate?" Mercy and Owen stand on the steps of Smokin' Elliot's. Mercy has a takeout container in her hands.

I run over to them, grabbing them both and hugging them tight.

And then I start to cry.

Chapter Thirteen

I thought back to my last conversation with Mike.

The sun was getting low. Orange reflected off the waves of the Starling like flames. I sat on the edge of the dock at Camp Clearwater, my bedroll in my lap, leaning against my bags. My parents would be here to pick me up any minute. They were late, as usual. Most of the other campers had gone. Owen's parents had come for him at the crack of dawn. Mercy's came not long after. My parents were always late. Which suited me fine. I glanced down at the sleeve of my shirt–blue. Fourth year. I wasn't ready for it to be over.

"Hey, Nate." Mike appeared beside me, kicking off his flip-flops. He took a seat, letting his feet dangle in the water. "Thought maybe you'd left without saying goodbye."

"Nope," was all I said.

He tugged at my shirt and grinned. "You'll have to trade this in for red next year."

Fifth year. Red shirt. My palms began to sweat.

"And once you finish fifth year, you can apply to be a counselor, with me!" said Mike.

I glanced at his bright-white counselor's T-shirt, the neon-orange whistle hanging from his neck. Being a counselor with Mike was my dream. But it meant getting through fifth year to do it.

"Hello?" said Mike. "Earth to Nate?"

"Yeah," I sighed. "Sweet."

Mike raised an eyebrow. "What's the matter with you, man?"

"Nothing."

Mike laughed. "*Nothing*," he mocked. "Doesn't sound like nothing. Seriously, I thought you'd be stoked about graduating to red shirt."

I was dreading it. I'd been dreading it since first year.

"What if I fail?"

Mike laughed. "When have you failed at anything you've tried at Camp Clearwater?"

Never. I'd never failed at anything. But I'd never ridden any rapid above a Class Three. That would all change in fifth year. In fifth year we would take on Class Four.

"What if I can't handle the Nebula?" I asked.

Mike frowned and looked out at the water. "I'm not going to tell you you're ready for it, Nate. Because only you can decide that. You have to do what's right for you. But what I can tell you is, you're the best paddler I've got. That's a fact. And if you can't handle the Nebula, then none of them can."

"You think that?"

"Darn right I do," said Mike. "You're better than anyone I've taught. And you're definitely better than me. And if I could get through the Nebula, then I know you can."

I didn't believe that. But I liked that he said it all the same. He made me feel like I could really do it if I wanted to.

That was the last time I saw Mike face-to-face.

Downtown, Owen, Mercy and I sit on the banks of the Starling, the night turning the river to ink. The lights of the town spill over the bridge above us. That last conversation with Mike plays in my mind over and over. He was always trying to make me feel like I could do anything. And I believed him because I really thought Mike could do anything.

Like survive in the woods alone.

And now they've called off the search.

"I can't believe it," Owen says, barely loud enough to hear. The three of us have been sitting in silence for what feels like an hour. When we found each other outside the BBQ Shack, Mr. Evans left us to go talk to the sheriff. None of us are processing the news about Mike very well.

"I just don't understand what this means," says Mercy.

I throw a stick into the black water. "It means they've stopped looking."

"Yeah but....does that mean they think he's–"

"Yes," I say bitterly. "It means they think he's dead."

"Nate!" Owen says, horrified. But it's the truth. The police have given up on him. Because they don't know Mike Elliot.

"What do *you* think?" Mercy asks me.

"I think he's still out there," I say. "I think he's waiting for someone to find him."

Owen frowns at me, reading my thoughts. "Someone."

I nod. "Someone like me."

Owen's chin drops to his chest. He shakes his head. "Nate, you can't just go out there looking for him."

"No one else will."

"You said Mr. Evans is talking to the police. They know about these goons you saw. Maybe that will help."

"It's not enough," I tell him. "They aren't even *looking* for Mike anymore. Catching the guys that did this to him doesn't matter if he isn't here to see it!"

"What are you going to do?" says Owen. "Take on the whole Starling, the Black Hole, *by yourself*?"

"Not by himself." Mercy gets to her feet, half of her face lit by the streetlights. "I'll go with you, Nate."

"Thanks, Mercy."

Owen groans, shaking his head again. "Well, I can't let you two idiots go out there by yourselves."

"You don't have to come, Owen," I tell him.

"Yes, I do," he says. "I was in first aid with both of you, and I know neither of you can remember how to do CPR right."

He has a point. And I know he's not just worried about first aid. He doesn't think Mercy and I will be able to make the responsible decisions. That's always been Owen's job.

"I guess," says Mercy, "all we need now are some kayaks."

I nod. "We need to get back to camp."

"Let's just hope that my car is ready," says Mercy.

Chapter Fourteen

It doesn't take long to walk to Higgins Autobody. It looks different in the dark. This afternoon it was bustling and noisy with mechanics working on cars. Now it's quiet, not a soul in sight. But the sign is still glowing, and there's a light on in the main office.

As we walk up to the door, I notice a van parked out front.

I stop.

"What?" asks Owen.

"That's Mr. Evans's van," I say. "He's supposed to be at the sheriff's."

Mercy shrugs and opens the door to the main office. "Maybe he got a rock to the windshield too. Come on."

Inside, a vending machine hums. Mercy hits the service bell, but no one answers.

"Are we sure it's still open?" asks Owen.

Mercy rolls her eyes. "It says so on the door, doesn't it?"

Behind the counter is a hallway with a couple closed doors. Closets and offices, I figure. To my right, an open door leads into the garage. I can hear voices coming from there. I wander over and poke my head in. Mercy's car sits at the far end of the garage. The windshield is fixed. Several other cars are parked beside it. No mechanics at work.

The voices are coming from the back of the garage. I can see an office there, with big glass windows. There's a light on, and I can see men inside.

Mr. Evans.

He stands with his arms folded, leaning against the wall. In front of him, a round old man is shouting at someone else in the room. I take a couple careful steps toward them, making sure I can't be seen. As I get closer I can read the name on the door. Bob Higgins. The shouting is getting louder.

"I thought I made myself perfectly clear the last time," he roars.

He's shouting at two people sitting in chairs. I can't see their faces. One of them must say something, because Mr. Higgins slams his fist on the desk between them.

"Then why has Steve Evans come all the way here to tell me you idiots nearly got another kid drowned on the river?"

My heart stops. Mike.

No. He said *another.* He's talking about me.

Mr. Evans opens the door, and I can hear his words easily. "I don't want to be here for this, Bob. I just came to tell you that it's over. I can't do this anymore."

Mr. Higgins turns on Mr. Evans. "You accepted the money just fine. You got what you wanted."

"I said you could dump what you like on Clearwater land so long as no one found out about it," says Mr. Evans.

A queasiness fills my stomach. He *knew* about the ponds?

"Now I've got one camper missing and another nearly drowned," he says. "I'm sorry, Bob, but I won't keep doing this if it means my kids are at risk."

He knew. He knew what happened to Mike before I even told him.

"If you talk, you think Sheriff Nichols will just ignore the fact that you were making money while the whole town searched for poor lost Mike Elliot?"

"You can have the money back." Mr. Evans's voice is high, panicked.

He never went to Sheriff Nichols! He kept telling me not to come with him. I thought it was because he didn't want to push me, like his note in my file said. But no. He didn't want me to come because he was never planning to go to Sheriff Nichols at all.

Mr. Higgins grins. "We've been in business together a lot of years, Evans. You got a hundred large to just hand back?"

A hundred thousand dollars. Mr. Evans, what have you done?

"Nate?"

All the heads in the office turn at the sound of my name. Mercy stands in the door to the garage. We've been spotted.

Time to run.

I turn on my heels and race back for Owen and Mercy as Mr. Evans calls my name.

"Stop them!" bellows Mr. Higgins, and the two men he was shouting at jump to their feet. I look back. It's Ed and Dale. They tear out of the office, chasing after me.

"What's going on?" shouts Owen.

"Run! We have to run!"

Mercy and Owen don't need to be told twice. The three of us take off at a sprint out of the body shop. We run for the bridge, Ed and Dale still on our tail.

"The trees!" I shout. "Quick!"

We plow into the darkness of the pines. It's so black I can barely see the branches that whip my face. But I can hear Ed and Dale behind us, crashing through the forest like elephants.

I slam into a fallen log and fly forward into the dirt. Owen and Mercy tumble on top of me.

"Quiet, quiet," I whisper urgently.

The three of us lie there, listening to Ed and Dale stumbling and swearing as they try to make their way.

"Where'd they go?" says one of them. "Did you see which way they went?"

"I can't see anything in this place."

Their voices are getting quieter. They're moving away from us.

We wait, flat on our stomachs, until there's nothing left to hear. After what feels like ages, the three of us agree the coast is clear.

We trudge back toward the Starling and follow it, knowing the river will take us to Clearwater.

"What the heck was that?" Owen whispers as we walk. "Nate, what happened back there?"

"What happened?" I almost laugh. The rage coursing through me is too much to handle. "Mr. Evans is a liar, that's what happened."

"What?" says Mercy.

"Mr. Evans knew who was responsible for Mike's disappearance all this time," I tell her. "He was getting paid to let those jerks dump their junk on Camp Clearwater property. He never went to the sheriff."

Mr. Evans betrayed Mike.

Betrayed all of us.

Chapter Fifteen

“Nate, we have to go to the sheriff,” says Owen.

Owen, Mercy and I are still making our way along the dark shores of the Starling, trying to get back to Camp Clearwater.

“There’s no time,” I say.

Owen grabs me by the elbow. “Nate, this is serious. We need to go to the police. We need adults in on this.”

“He’s right,” agrees Mercy.

“Adults?” I shove Owen off me. “Which adults do you want help from? The police?

The guys who were supposed to find Mike and just gave up? Or Mr. Evans, the guy whose entire job is to take care of Clearwater and its campers? What exactly is it you think the adults are going to do to help us, Owen?"

"Nate," Mercy begins, but I don't want to hear it. I'm so mad. So furious it's all I can do to keep from breaking down into tears.

"Mike is out there!" I scream. "He's out there, and no one is looking for him. We can't wait for the adults to sit around talking and lying and coming up with a million different ways to tell us there's nothing they can do."

Mercy and Owen look away, unable to meet my eyes. Because they know I'm right. They know the only way Mike will be found is if we find him ourselves.

"I'm done waiting, Mercy," I say. "I'm not letting these guys get away with what they've done. We need to find Mike–*now*."

"How?" demands Owen. "By going through the Black Hole? Nate, that's insane."

"You said you would come with me!"

"I know what I said!" he shouts. "But now we're getting chased by goons! Mr. Evans is part of some crazy crime scheme! I mean, Nate, it's barely the start of summer. The winter storms will have brought all kinds of trees down and other strainers that no one's cleared yet. It's too dangerous!"

"Then don't come with us!" I shout.

Owen looks at Mercy. She doesn't say anything, just chews on a nail. She meets Owen's eyes but won't look at me. She agrees with him. The Black Hole scares them. And I don't blame them. The Black Hole is a monster. It nearly killed me once.

I sigh, facing the river. "You're right. It is too dangerous. When we get back to camp, you guys can go find Raina. Tell her to take you to the sheriff."

"What about you?" asks Mercy.

My eyes burn. "I'm going to find Mike." Because no one else will. But the idea of doing it alone, without my friends, makes me more frightened than ever.

"Nate–"

"Just give me enough time to get my gear together before you go to Raina, okay?"

Mercy shakes her head, "Nate, we aren't going to let you go alone."

"Mercy, this is something I just have to do. Mike would do it for me."

She doesn't argue that. She knows he would. He'd do it for any of us.

"Well," says Mercy, with a clap of her hands, "we'd better hurry up then." She marches past me. "We've got a lot of gear to get ready if we're going to do this, and it's getting late."

"What?"

"Yeah," says Owen, "what?"

"It's like you said," she says, without looking back. "Mike would do it for any of us. So I don't see we have much of a choice."

I glance over at Owen, whose chin is in his chest.

"Owen," I say, "you don't have to–"

"Just shut up," he says, following after Mercy, "before I change my mind about this."

By the time we make it to Camp Clearwater, it's late. Most of the lights are out except for the office's porch light and the floodlight by the flagpole. And headlights. Three sets of headlights, parked on the lawn.

"Guys," whispers Mercy, crouched behind a rack of kayaks. Owen and I crouch with her, and she points at the cars. "That's the men from the garage."

Ed and Dale lean against a truck.

"They must be waiting for us," says Owen. "They knew we'd come back here."

My anger deepens. *I wonder who gave them* that *idea.*

"How are we supposed to get to the cabin to get our gear?"

The lights from their cars spill onto the beach. If we step out from behind the boat racks, they'll spot us instantly. We're stuck here.

"We can't just wait here," says Owen. "They could stand there all night."

The door to the main office bursts open, and Mr. Evans steps onto the porch. "I said get out of here!" He holds the door open, shouting at whoever's inside. "If I have to ask again, I'm calling the sheriff."

Bob Higgins saunters out of the office. He says something to Mr. Evans I can't quite hear from this far away. But whatever it is, it makes Mr. Evans deflate. Higgins struts over to his car and shouts orders at Ed and Dale. "When those kids turn up, you call me."

Ed and Dale nod as the car door slams and Bob Higgins drives away. Mr. Evans sits on the porch, his head in his knees.

"Why isn't he calling the sheriff like he said he would?" Mercy whispers.

My jaw tightens. "Because he took their money. He's a part of this whole thing. If he calls the sheriff, he'll get arrested just like the rest of them."

"What are we supposed to do now?" asks Mercy.

My eyes fall on the equipment shack behind us. I remember what happened the night Sarah Bauer challenged Mike to a midnight run of the Nebula.

"I think we need a flare."

Chapter Sixteen

Owen and I crouch in the racks of kayaks, our eyes on the trees.

"Maybe she couldn't get in," says Owen.

Maybe. If Mercy couldn't get into the shed to get the flares, I'm out of ideas. This is the best plan we've got. It needs to work. For Mike's sake, it needs to.

"I don't like this," Owen goes on. "Even if we do pull this off, we're heading out on the Starling at night, Nate. We won't be able to see anything."

"We just have to get downriver," I tell him. "Just far enough that we're hidden in the dark and out of sight, and then we'll make camp for the night."

He shakes his head. "I still don't like it."

Of course not. But what other choice is there?

I glance back to where Bob's goons are sitting with Mr. Evans. Ed and Dale have been smoking and laughing, sitting on the hood of the truck, ignoring Mr. Evans completely. Mr. Evans hasn't looked up from his knees. I stare at him, trying to understand how he could have fooled me–fooled all of us–into thinking he was our friend for so long. Then again, maybe he didn't think he was fooling us. Maybe he really did care. I don't know how much money a camp director makes. Maybe it isn't much. Maybe the amount of money Bob Higgins was offering was just too much for him to turn down. Maybe he really needed it. Maybe he was desperate.

I growl, shaking my head. It doesn't matter what Mr. Evans may have needed. What matters is he lied. What matters is he put us all at risk. What matters is Mike is missing. And for what? A few extra bucks in his pocket?

Why do I love it? Mr. Evans's voice is inside my head. Our first riverside picnic in our first week at Camp Clearwater. *Because nothing gets your heart pumping the way the river does. There's no greater joy than remembering how small I am in the grand scheme of things. No greater reminder than the feel of that white water tossing around my little boat. And knowing that I can get through it.*

I wonder when he forgot all that. Or if he ever even meant it.

Suddenly I see Ed slide off the hood of the truck. He's pointing toward the tree line.

"What the hell?" shouts Dale.

Owen and I look to the trees, and there it is, the bright-orange glow of a flare. Not just one flare. Mercy must have lit a whole box. The blaze is blinding. Ed and Dale are shouting at each other. Mr. Evans gets to his feet.

"C'mon, Dale!" shouts Ed, and they take off toward the trees.

"You stay away from those kids!" bellows Mr. Evans, taking off after them.

"Now," I tell Owen.

The two of us sprint for the cabin, bursting in the door and frantically grabbing all our gear–neoprene skirts, PFDs, carabiners, helmets, throw bag, granola bars, Mercy's crackers.

"Got everything?"

"I don't know!" snaps Owen. "We usually have days to plan this kind of thing, Nate! I don't know what I have here–this is insanity."

He's right. If this were a camp excursion, we'd have checklists and counselors like Raina or Mike checking everything we packed, ensuring we were well prepared. This is reckless.

"It'll have to do," I tell him. "Mercy's waiting by the water. We have to go."

Owen scoops up what he can in his arms and heads for the door. I move to follow and realize I've forgotten Mike's river knife. It's sitting on the desk, black and sleek. I snatch it and run.

Owen and I jog toward the water, where Mercy is waiting with three kayaks ready to go.

"Do you have everything?" she whispers.

"We hope so," I say, handing her a helmet.

"That's reassuring."

"Where are they?" asks Owen.

She points toward the trees. There's a small grassfire burning now. "They didn't see me. They're trying to control the flames, kicking dirt and stuff. We'd better hurry though. It looks like they're close to snuffing it out."

As quick as we can, we strap on our gear.

Mercy grabs Owen by the arm. "Did you bring my water shoes?"

"I couldn't find them."

"I can't go without my water shoes."

"There they are!" Behind us, Ed and Dale emerge from the trees by the flagpole, Mr. Evans behind them.

"Nate!" I hear him shout. "Nate, stop!"

But there's no way to stop now.

"Forget the shoes, Mercy!" I scream, dumping the rest of the gear into the boat and shoving off into the river.

"Nate!" Mr. Evans yells as the three men run toward us. "Mercy! Owen! It's too dangerous!"

I'm in the water. Floating on the Starling. Free of dry land. If we can get just a little downriver, we'll be hidden in the dark. I dip my paddle into the water, ready to disappear–

Mercy screams behind me.

Ed and Dale have charged into the water, grabbing onto the back of Mercy's kayak.

"Mercy!" shouts Owen.

I circle back, digging my paddle into the water as hard and as fast as I can. When I'm close enough, I take a swing at Ed, the staff of my paddle connecting with his nose, and he falls back with a groan.

Mercy brings her paddle up, driving it into Dale's chin. His head cranks back, and his massive body falls with a splash.

"Go, Mercy!" I shout, taking off down the river. "Quick!"

"Kids!" Mr. Evans stands knee-deep in the Starling. "Come back! It's not safe!"

But there is no going back. Not after what Mr. Evans has done.

The only way is forward, to where the Starling takes us.

And, hopefully, it takes us to Mike.

Chapter Seventeen

It's morning on the shores of the Starling. The world is cold with dew. My skin is covered in goose bumps, and I'm damp from sleeping in the twigs and dirt and grass. I really wish I was wearing my dry top, to shield me from all this wet. But in the frenzy to get out of Camp Clearwater, I didn't pack it.

The sun peeks over the trees. It's early, and I don't see a cloud in the sky. It's a good day to be on the river.

Mercy sits on a rock at the water's edge, laying out her gear. When I went to bed last night, she was sitting in that same spot. "Someone should keep a lookout in case they come after us," she'd said.

"Have you been up all night?" I ask, taking a seat beside her.

She shakes her head. "I slept a couple hours."

"Mercy, you really should have got more rest."

"Excuse me if I couldn't get a little shut-eye while we're on the run from criminal masterminds."

I raise an eyebrow. "Masterminds?"

She grins. "Well, whatever they are."

I look at all the gear, carefully organized into piles–inner layer, outer layer and safety equipment.

"Have everything?" I ask.

"No. I'd like a dry top–it's so cold."

"Yeah. Me too."

"What about you?" she asks. "Are you ready for this?"

"I kind of have to be."

She nods. "First up, the Nebula."

The water froths and crests in mighty waves. Owen, Mercy and I float in our boats in an eddy on the edge of the rapids. The hydraulics of the Nebula are enough to stun us all into silence. Massive holes, surging foam piles, giant rocks. This is the final test for Camp Clearwater paddlers.

"You swam through that?" Owen asks, jaws gaping.

"Splashed helplessly through is more like it," I say, remembering the power of the water.

Mercy squints, reading the river as best she can from our vantage point.

"What are you thinking?" I ask her.

She points her paddle at the right side of the river. "See over there? The way that water's moving? It's got the most volume. It'll be fast, straightforward, fewest obstacles. Looks like the best line to me."

I watch the water. Mercy's right. The biggest holes–where the water drops suddenly and churns back in on itself–seem to be on the left. If we keep right, we can avoid them and ride the flow volume through the Nebula in the shortest amount of time.

I nod. "Looks good to me."

Owen shakes his head. He looks like he's going to be sick. "I mean...I guess?"

That's as close to a thumbs-up as I figure we're going to get from Owen. Mercy seems to think the same thing because she takes off into the Nebula, her boat riding the current like a roller coaster, popping up on the crests of each mighty wave.

Owen's next, following Mercy.

But I don't move.

My hands begin to shake as the roar of the Nebula fills my ears. I remember how it tried to crush me. And suddenly I'm back to being a little kid, the white water of the Black Hole pulling me under, pulling me to my death.

You survived it! a voice inside me shouts. *You've survived it twice!*

I tighten my grip on my paddle. This time I'm in control.

I join the current, my boat peeling off with the flow. The world races by in a blur. The current is fast, so fast I barely have time to react to the obstacles that come up at me. Rocks and branches. I just squeak my way through, mostly by luck. This water is too fast. I'm not ready for this.

Breathe.

Focus.

In the kayak, the waves seem even bigger than they did when I swam, raising me up so I can nearly touch the branches of the treetops and swooping me low so that it's like the river has no bottom.

And suddenly I'm laughing.

Water crashes over my boat and pushes me forward, the rush of the Starling carrying me on an amazing ride. This is why we do this. This is what it's all about.

I scream into the air, egging on the Nebula to bring it on. Do its worst.

The Starling is mine–I am its master.

And then I see it. A massive hole–a whirlpool of churning, bubbling white water–just ahead.

Owen makes his way toward it, but I don't like his angle. His best bet is to drive into the hole, shooting straight through. But he's approaching at a thirty-degree angle, and fast. "Owen, straighten out!" I shout.

He tries, but he's too slow, and I watch him go over, hitting the foam pile at the bottom, just before the boil line.

The kayak flips. He's stuck where the downstream water collides with the water rushing back to fill the space.

"Owen!" I scream.

He can't hear me. He's under the kayak. I paddle as hard as I can, driving into the hole, careful to avoid knocking his boat. I spin around, balancing on the boil before the current picks back up.

"Owen!" I scream, tapping his boat with the front of mine. "Owen, grab on!"

He's been under so long. Why doesn't he come up?

Suddenly a hand shoots out from the white foam and grabs hold of my kayak. I hang on, keeping as steady as I can manage while Owen rights himself. He gasps, coughing and sputtering.

"Are you all right?" I shout over the thunder.

"I'm fine," he says.

I wait for him, battling the water that wants to carry me off. Owen pops his boat out of the boil line and shoots downriver after Mercy.

She has eddied out where the current breaks off and the water is calm, by the right bank. When Owen and I finally make it to her, all of us are panting, breathing hard.

Owen's cheeks spread into a smile, and Mercy and I can't help but smile too.

Owen throws back his head, screaming into the sky and pumping his paddle in the air. Mercy and I join him, cheering and laughing because we can't believe we did it.

"Should they just give us our counselor shirts now or what?" Mercy exclaims, laughing.

"Seriously," says Owen. "Who needs fifth year? We *got* this!"

We all laugh and try to catch our breath, but the excitement is short-lived. Because it doesn't take us long to remember that the Nebula was supposed to be the easy part of this mission. And it wasn't easy at all.

Now we have to take on the Black Hole.

Chapter Eighteen

The Black Hole looks like the collision of universes.

Owen, Mercy and I stand on the edge of a cliff, looking down into it. After the Nebula, we decided to scout ahead. We walked along the Starling until we found it. Now, seeing the rapids for the first time since I battled it as a kid, I feel my knees trembling.

There's no blue water. No dark, calm spots peppered amid the foam. It's just white, churning, angry waves, massive holes and who knows what obstacles hidden under all that chaos.

"Jeez, Nate," Mercy says, getting down on her knees to look closer. "I don't know. I don't–I'm not even sure where to begin."

I know what she means. It's just a mess. I can't tell where the flows are, can't understand the lines through–if there even are any lines through. I watch the water, trying to read it. The river makes a hard right turn through the canyon, forcing the water against the rock face. I can just make out all the boulders and undercut rocks from up here. The water has been carving away at all that for centuries.

"There," Mercy says finally. "See through the middle there? That's the best line, right?"

I shake my head. The Black Hole isn't like the Nebula. We can't approach it the same way. "We can't just blitz through it," I tell her. "We tried that with the Nebula, and it was too fast. I barely had time to react to obstacles in the way. Down there, especially with that turn, we need all the reaction time we can get."

"What are you thinking?" asks Owen.

"We don't go straight through. We zigzag, eddy to eddy."

Mercy nods. "To slow us down."

"Exactly. And we can stick together more easily."

"You really think he's down there?" Owen asks. "In that?"

I don't have an answer. He had to come out somewhere. And we won't be able to find him unless we follow.

I bob in the water, working up the courage to head into the Black Hole. It's been five years since I was here last. And the memories are flooding back in a rush that makes my palms sweat. The fear. The crushing, impossible weight of the river. The ache of the water filling my lungs.

Mercy and Owen sit just behind me. They've both gone pale. The Nebula was one thing, but this is something else. This is something almost supernatural.

I turn and nod at them. "For Mike."

They nod back. "For Mike."

And with that I paddle forward.

Once I'm in the current, the speed is too much. I'm out of control, and I've only just started. Water swamps the front of my boat, and I shoot through the canyon like a bullet, my arms burning as I paddle like a maniac, fighting the river.

Don't fight it, Mike says inside my head. *Go with it.*

But the river doesn't want me to go with it. It wants to toss me. Wants to drown me. I hit a major drop, unlike any I've ever gone over before, and I can't keep my balance. I spiral over, my whole body upside down as the water crashes around me. I spin like a top, and suddenly the whole boat is underwater, the downstream flow pushing me to the riverbed. And then the boat's free, shooting to the surface. I'm spat out of a foam pile, sailing into another drop. I swallow water. Panic overwhelms me.

And then I'm upright.

I growl against the weight of the waves crashing down, the boat bucking beneath me as more waves try to drive me upward.

And I can see the bend in the river.

See the canyon wall coming up fast.

And the rocks.

So many rocks.

I try to angle the kayak away, the back of it scraping the first rock, knocking me sideways. I slam into the second one, ricocheting off it like a pinball. I can't control this. I can't tame it. I'm a leaf on the current. I'm driftwood.

I slam into the rock face, water pinning me, and I angle myself as best I can to break free and join the current. I manage to move again, flying down the river, more waves swamping me.

And then a boulder, big as a house, comes into my path. I can see the way the water flows around it.

No, not around. The water is flowing through. The water has cut its way through the boulder. It's a sieve.

And I'm headed straight for it.

The kayak shoots beneath the boulder, but my body collides with the rock. Water crashes against my back like a freight train, the boat threatening to pull me under the rock. I can't move. I can't get out.

This is how people drown.

This is how people die.

This is how I'm going to die.

And then a rope—a bright-yellow rope—lands between my face and the rock. I can barely see it over the pounding of the water. I've imagined it. I'm dreaming of a way out of this.

The rope hits my nose as the water jostles it around. I'm not dreaming. Mercy or Owen must have tossed it to me.

I grab hold of the rope, and the water swallows me up, taking me under in a thunder of bubbles. But the rope is taut in my hands. I can feel the water fighting me as the rope hauls me toward shore, against the pull of the current.

My head hits rock, and an arm wraps around my chest, holding me under my armpits, and I'm hauled out of the water.

I lie on my back, sopping wet and sputtering for air.

And a face looks over me.

A face I recognize.

"Nate? What the hell are you doing?"

Mike.

Chapter Nineteen

I sit up, my heart hammering, as I stare into a face I can't believe I'm seeing.

It's thinner than I remember. And hairier.

But it's Mike's face.

"Nate?" he says again.

I lunge for him, wrapping my arms around him and hugging him tightly to me. He reeks of body odor and dirt and river water. But he's here. He's really here. Alive. Like I knew he would be.

He winces, pulling back from me. "Easy, easy."

He grabs his knee, and when I look, I see that his leg below the shin is broken, the bone poking through the skin.

"Jesus, Nate," he says, tears welling in his eyes. "I can't believe it's really you."

"Mike," I say, not believing the sound of his name. "Mike, what happened to you?"

He motions at the leg. "This," he says simply. "Caught a sieve, just like you. Fell out of my kayak and broke my leg. It was all I could do to get to this ledge."

"You've just been here this whole time?"

"Well, not right here." He nods back into the rock face, and I can see where he's been sleeping–between a boulder and the rock wall. How many cold nights has he spent here? In so much pain.

"I told them," I say angrily. "I told them you were alive! I told them!"

He points up at the sky. "Hard to see me through all that." I follow his pointed finger and see what he means. Branches and trees hang over the cliff face. Even if he could somehow signal the search helicopters, with his limited mobility there would be no way for them to see through all that.

"Mike, I know what happened," I say. "I know about Bob Higgins and his toxic waste pools on Clearwater property."

"Higgins," Mike snarls. "His henchmen chased me when I caught them. I sprinted back for camp, and they chased me in their trucks. The only way I could get away was to grab one of the kayaks and take the plunge."

I'm about to tell him about Mr. Evans, but I stop myself. After everything he's been through, I wonder if I should wait. He's so weak and so injured. I don't have the heart to add more pain.

"Thank god I had a bag of trail mix with me," he goes on.

"That's all you've been eating?"

"*Was* eating. I ran out yesterday morning. Figured I'd have to turn to bugs soon." He laughs, but it's a sad laugh, and his eyes well up again and he grabs me, hugging me tightly.

"Wait," I say, backing away. "I have something for you." I fish into my pocket and pull out the knife. He smiles, taking it in his hands like he can't believe it's real. "When I saw that, I knew something was wrong."

"God, what are you doing here, Nate? What are you doing, trying to take on the Black Hole?"

"We came to find you!" I tell him.

"We?"

And then I hear them, over the roar of the Starling–Owen and Mercy shouting my name. They come running along the bank, hopping over rocks and picking their way over boulders. But Mike and I are too hidden–they'll never see us.

"One sec," I tell Mike, and I pop up, maneuvering my way over another rock so Mercy and Owen can see me. "Guys!" I shout. "Over here!"

Mercy and Owen climb up onto my rock. "Nate!" Mercy cries, hugging me. "What happened!? We saw you getting dragged toward shore and–"

"Guys," I say, interrupting Mercy. I motion down to where Mike is sitting.

Owen's and Mercy's jaws drop.

Mike grins. "*I said boom chick-a boom!*"

I laugh at the camp song, but Owen and Mercy don't move.

Because they can't believe we did it.

We found Mike Elliot.

Chapter Twenty

Getting Mike back to civilization was an ordeal. Mercy and Owen went for help, and I stayed with Mike. Eventually Search and Rescue showed up with helicopters and boats, and Mike was airlifted to Guilford Falls hospital. They kept him in for four days before they finally let him go home.

And I was there every day with Owen and Mercy.

The sheriff took our statements, and it didn't take long for the police to arrest Ed, Dale and Bob Higgins.

And Mr. Evans.

When they arrested Mr. Evans, we really weren't sure what would happen to Camp Clearwater. Mercy was worried they'd shut down the camp entirely.

But thank goodness for Raina.

I am sitting on the edge of the dock at Camp Clearwater, the sun hanging low in the sky.

"Nate!" Raina calls. She is standing on the shore, a bunch of first-year kayaks strewn all over the beach. "Would you mind putting these away for me?"

"No problem." I'm happy to help in any way I can. Since she became camp director and took over for Mr. Evans, she's been pulled in a million directions, trying to do everything at once. Not only is she doing Mr. Evans's job, but she's still doing hers.

"Thanks, Nate," she says with a smile. "I'll save you a brownie."

I set to work putting the boats to bed, my stomach grumbling. It's dinnertime, and I can smell spaghetti sauce on the air.

"Nate!" Mike waves over by the flagpole, making his way down to the water. He's got a cast on his injured leg, crutches. But he is moving pretty well, considering. He is wearing his white counselor shirt and looks more like his old self. "You want some help, man?"

"It's okay, I got it."

"Nate," he says, rolling his eyes. "It's a broken leg. I'm not dying."

"Fine then." I toss a paddle at him, and he drops one of his crutches just in time to catch it. He wobbles, and I worry he's going to fall. But he keeps his balance and laughs.

We work together, stacking the kayaks neatly on the racks. We're quiet as we work, neither one of us talking. It's not like Mike to be this quiet. Something's on his mind.

"What's up?" I ask him finally.

He puts down his armful of paddles and sighs. "I saw Mr. Evans today."

"What?" Mr. Evans is in jail.

Mike nods. "I needed to talk to him. To understand, you know?"

"What's to understand?" I don't care what Mr. Evans has to say for himself. He nearly got all of us killed.

Mike shrugs. "Turns out the money wasn't for him," he says.

"Sure it wasn't."

"No, Nate, really. I asked Raina, and she confirmed what he told me. The camp has no money. Apparently, Clearwater is just barely staying afloat. Mr. Evans thought the money from Bob Higgins could help him save the camp."

I let that sink in for a minute. A part of me wants that to be good enough. Wants that to be a reasonable explanation for what Mr. Evans did. But then I think of Mike sitting alone between those rocks for so many days, hoping to be rescued. I think of the raging waters of the Black Hole. And it isn't. It isn't good enough at all.

"He seemed really sorry," Mike says.

"I'll bet he is."

Mike nods and picks up the paddles, stacking them against the racks.

"What?" I ask him. "Are you saying you forgive him?"

He shrugs. "I don't know. Maybe not forgive. But I understand a little bit better."

"Well, I don't," I say. "I don't understand at all."

"Come on, Nate. Think about how much you love this place. How much we all do. Are you really telling me you wouldn't try anything to save it?"

"I wouldn't do what he did."

"No," agrees Mike. "But still, he did it because he loves this place as much as we do. We're all just between swims, aren't we?"

Between swims. It's something Mr. Evans used to remind us about whenever we went out on the Starling. Every time you're in a kayak, it's only until the next time the rapids beat you.

Maybe Mike's got a point. Camp Clearwater has been a home to all of us, a place to find ourselves. And Mr. Evans wanted to keep that safe. But he did it all wrong. And he ended up making us less safe than ever. Maybe someday I can be as understanding as Mike. But it is going to take me a while.

"So," I ask Mike, "if there's no money, what does that mean for Clearwater?"

"Ah, Raina's already got a bunch of fundraising events planned. You know how organized she is. If anyone can get Clearwater back on track, it's Raina."

I nod. Raina will take care of it.

"Don't worry, Nate." Mike grins. "You'll wear the white shirt soon enough."

I smile. Fifth year is almost over. I ran the Nebula again with the red shirts and passed. It was easier the second time, with all my fellow campers there supporting one another. More fun and less frightening than that day we went to find Mike.

Raina offered me a job next summer as counselor. A white shirt like Mike. And not just me. She offered the same thing to Mercy and Owen. We all said we'd be back. Assuming Raina can figure out how to keep Clearwater operating.

"Mike!"

We turn and see Sarah Bauer waving from the head-office building. She beckons for Mike to come.

I glance at him sideways. "So Sarah Bauer, eh?"

"What?"

I shake my head. "Just a surprise is all."

Mike tries not to blush, grinning like an idiot. "Ah, you'll understand it someday. After all, if you can get over your fear of the Starling enough to come find me, you can get over your other fear."

He hobbles off to join her, leaving me alone by the stacks.

"What other fear?" I call after him.

"Girls!" he says.

I frown. I think about pointing out that I talk to Mercy just fine, but then he'll think I've got a crush on her. Which I don't.

I turn back to the Starling, watching the setting sun glitter off the waves. So next year I'll be on my river again. The river I love. Wearing a white shirt.

Next to Mike.

M.J. McIsaac is the author of several books for young people, including *Underhand* from the Orca Sports collection. She has a master's degree in writing for children from the University of Winchester in the UK. M.J. currently lives with her family in Whitby, Ontario.

Check out another great
Orca Sports title by M.J. McIsaac

9781459804166 PB

Chapter One

Looking at the world from behind a cage does something to the brain. You see a tiger pacing back and forth and people say he's bored. I don't know about that. I think he's probably just fired up. Ready to break out and take no prisoners. That's how it is for me anyway, when I put on that helmet and see the world from behind those bars.

My cheeks feel like they're the surface of the sun. I can feel the sweat beneath my pads, dripping down my back. I'm soaked.

My muscles are burning, and I push my feet as fast as they can go. My limbs feel like rubber.

The ball is mine, safely nestled in the pocket of my stick while I barrel for the net. There's a thumping behind me, the steady pounding of the left creaseman coming to stop me.

"Look who you got, Nick!" Coach is screaming from the bench.

Out of the corner of my eye, I see my teammate tearing up the left side. That's who I got. But I don't need him. Coach'll see–*I've* got this.

And then he's hitting me, the left crease. My right shoulder tenses as he swats at my stick with his.

"Nick!" my teammate screams. "Over here!"

I ignore him. The net is calling my name.

I drop my stick and rip an underhand shot, bottom right–their goalie can't block it. And then a body, the left crease, cross-checks me on my right side and I'm knocked off my feet.

The whistle blows. Practice is over.

I lie there, staring at the arena's ceiling. Banners with our team's name on them, *Maplehurst Vikings*, hang down from the rafters. Coach is gonna kill me. My lungs swell until they're ready to burst. I try to ignore the tingling where my shoulder bit the concrete.

"Nick!" My teammate stands over me and takes off his helmet. I see the shaved-head silhouette of Markus, my brother. A bead of sweat from the end of his nose drops through my face mask, and I spit. "I was wide open. What the hell, man?"

He was. I spit again.

"Markus!" shouts Coach Preston from the bench. "Get changed, then come see me."

I'm a little relieved Coach didn't ask for me. Then again, he's said plenty to me today already. I guess he's finally given up.

Markus sighs and wipes his nose on the back of his sleeve. He nudges me with his foot. "Wait for me by the car."

When I don't say anything, he shakes his head and follows the rest of the Vikings to the change room.

I still lie there on the floor, staring up at the ceiling.